In the Realm of the

Never Fairies

The Secret World of Pixie Hollow

Text by Monique Peterson
Illustrated by The Disney Storybook Artists
Designed by Elizabeth Ryazantseva and Megan Krempels

Printed in the United States of America

First Edition

10 9 8 7 6 5 4 3 2 1

ISBN 0-7868-4765-4

Library of Congress Control Number: 2005906826

Visit www.disneyfairies.com

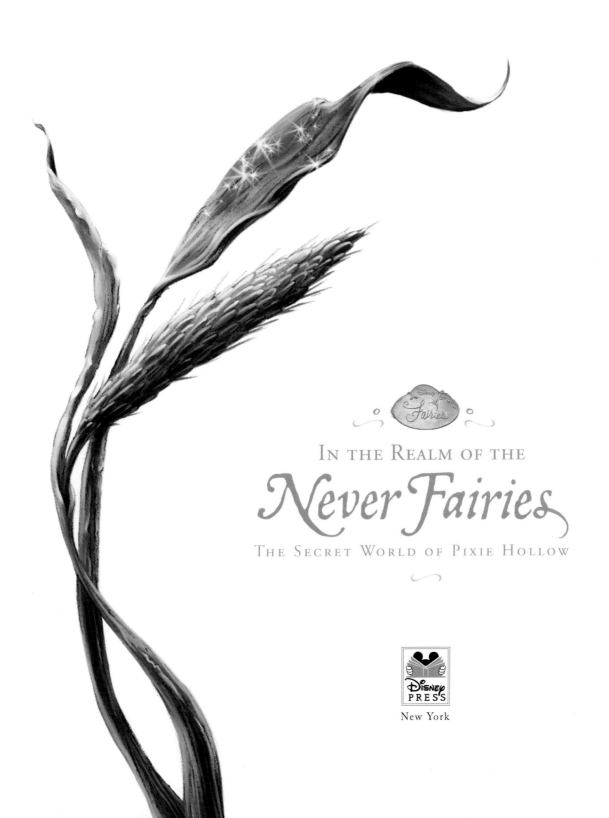

Disney Fairies

In the Realm of the
Never Fairies
The Secret World of Pixie Hollow

Disney PRESS

New York

Do You Believe in Fairies?

Have you ever felt a slight, shivering breeze whisper past your ear on a perfectly still day? Have you heard the faint chiming of tiny bells just before you fall asleep? Have you awoken suddenly in the darkest part of the night and seen a small dot of light dancing outside your window?

   Magic might be closer than you think. For just beyond the world you see, there is another world where the air shimmers with pixie dust. There nothing is impossible and magic happens every day.

   If you truly believe, clap your hands and follow that dancing dot of light. You might find yourself flying up beyond the stars, across a distant ocean, and into the heart of the most magical place of all . . .

...the Realm of the
Never Fairies

Pixie Hollow

Deep in the heart of Never Land lies a place called Pixie Hollow. Here, extraordinary creatures known as the Never fairies live, work, and play.

There are many kinds of fairies in the world, but Never fairies exist only on Never Land. Unlike their larger mainland-dwelling cousins, these fairies are tiny, and their magic comes not from wands or spells but from pixie dust.

Every fairy on Never Land has a talent. It is her calling in life—the thing she does best and loves best. Some fairies are experts in cricket-whistling. Some are skilled at turning berries into ink. There are fairies who spend all day soothing silkworms, or talking to trees, or summoning gusts of wind. There are as many different talents in Pixie Hollow as there are jobs to be done.

A male fairy is called a
SPARROW MAN.

HOW TO SPOT A NEVER FAIRY

Keep your ears tuned for the jingling sound of tiny bells—that is how fairies sound when they speak. Also, fairies smell like cinnamon. If you smell cinnamon rolls baking when there is no kitchen nearby, you may be in the presence of a fairy.

Many humans—or "Clumsies" as the fairies call them—never come in contact with fairies. In fact, adult humans cannot see them at all. They can feel fairies, however. A grown-up Clumsy will often mistake a pinch from a mischievous fairy for a mosquito bite.

Children, on the other hand, can spot fairies by their glow. The fairies' glow comes from pixie dust, which covers them like a dusting of sugar on a tea cake. Fairies can change the intensity and color of their glow depending on their moods. When a fairy is excited, her glow flares. If she blushes, it turns orange.

Pixie dust also gives Never fairies their ability to fly. Without it, fairies can fly no more than a few feet at a time.

Every fairy's wing pattern is unique. Like snowflakes, no two are the same.

Fairy wings do not feel pain.

Most fairies are approximately five inches tall.

Fairies normally glow lemon yellow edged with gold.

They weigh next to nothing. A fairy sitting in your palm feels no heavier than a handful of dandelion fluff.

The Ring of Belief

Although fairies are indifferent to adult Clumsies, they love children, for without them they would not exist. It is children's belief in them that keeps fairies alive. In turn, fairies keep children's belief in magic alive. The moment a child stops believing, a fairy will cease to exist. The only ones who can save a fading fairy are other children, who must clap to show they believe.

How Fairies Come to Be

All fairies are born from laughter. When a baby laughs for the first time, the laugh flies out into the world. It dances and flits about, looking for its home. At last, when it has arrived in the place it belongs, it explodes, turning into a fairy.

More often than not, the laugh will stay on the mainland (that is, in the world of Clumsies). There it may become a Great or Lesser Wanded fairy or a Giant Shimmering fairy. The laugh that turns into a Never fairy is a rare laugh indeed.

To become a Never fairy, the laugh makes a dangerous journey across a great ocean to reach Never Land. This can take up to several weeks, as many laughs get lost on the way. More importantly, Never Land must want the laugh. Only then will the island allow the laugh to arrive and find its place among the Never fairies.

Incomplete Fairies

Occasionally on its journey to Never Land, a piece of a laugh will crack off before it turns into a fairy. When that happens, the fairy arrives "incomplete." This may mean that the fairy's ear tips are missing, or that she has only a partial glow. Sometimes the fairy's incompleteness may be invisible, but is usually easily detected by her fellow fairies. For example, she might have no sense of etiquette, or be unable to pronounce the letter q.

Arrival

One of the most joyous occasions in Pixie Hollow is the arrival of a new fairy. No fairy or sparrow man wants to miss welcoming a new member to their community. And each and every one hopes that the newcomer will be part of their talent group.

The moment a Never fairy bursts forth from a laugh, the stray bits of laughter gather around her to become her Arrival Garment. The delicately woven strands of laughter are especially fragile. Once a fairy has received her wardrobe and no longer needs her Arrival Garment, it must be stored away carefully.

THE ANNOUNCEMENT

Upon the moment of her arrival in Pixie Hollow, a new fairy makes the Announcement, telling all the other fairies her name and her talent. The Announcement is a solemn moment for the other Never fairies and sparrow men, who all secretly hope that the new fairy will be part of their talent group.

Fairy Manners

Most fairies arrive knowing the rules of social etiquette. In general, Never fairies scoff at the habits and manners of Clumsies. When meeting another fairy for the first time, fairies never say, "Pleased to meet you." Instead they say, "I look forward to flying with you," or "Fly with you" for short.

Fairies have no use for titles such as "mister" and "miss." They call each other by their names only. One exception is Queen Clarion.

Clumsies say . . .	Fairies say . . .
"Pleased to meet you."	"Fly with you."
"See you later."	"Fly safely."
"I'm sorry."	"I'd fly backward if I could."
"Good-bye."	"Fly again soon."

Fairies never bow or curtsy, not even for the queen.

The Home Tree

In the heart of Pixie Hollow grows a towering maple tree that is home to almost all the Never fairies. The Home Tree is a magnificent sight to behold. Its trunk and limbs are aglow with light from hundreds of tiny windows and doorways, for each fairy and sparrow man has his or her own room here. Many fairies and sparrow men also have workshops in the great tree's limbs. The Home Tree is the center of the Never fairies' world, and they take great care of it.

With so many fairies living and working close together, they quickly learn to get along with each other. But once in a while, a problem arises that calls for the wisdom of Queen Clarion, the ruler of the Never fairies.

Queen Clarion

The Home Tree is the domain of Queen Clarion, the Never fairies' leader. While she oversees all life in Pixie Hollow, the Home Tree is where she spends most of her time.

Beloved by her subjects, Queen Clarion is wise and dignified in all her ways. She is a just ruler, and her greatest desire is to keep peace and unity among the fairies of Never Land.

The queen's ultimate concern is the health and well-being of her subjects. A good year is one in which few fairies are lost to disbelief. To this end, Queen Clarion is a cautious leader—she rarely takes risks that would jeopardize her subjects.

Queen Clarion has a special ability to bring out the best in all the fairies. The only creature who knows and understands the Never fairies better is Mother Dove. Ultimately, Queen Clarion is everything a fairy could wish for in a ruler.

The fairy crown is passed down from fairy queen to fairy queen.

One of Queen Clarion's favorite cloaks is an open-weave fern mantle.

TALENT:	Ruling over Pixie Hollow
LIKES:	Peace and prosperity
DISLIKES:	Hurricanes, fairy squabbles
FAVORITE FOOD:	Fig-chocolate cake
FAVORITE FLOWER:	Calla lily

The Lobby

The main entrance to the Home Tree is through the knothole door on the tree's west-facing side. The entrance opens into a grand lobby, which sparkles from top to bottom. This room is a source of great pride for the Never fairies, who have worked hard to make it beautiful.

The massive spiral staircase leads up to the second floor. It is mostly used by fairies whose wings are too wet to fly. Beyond the second level, fairies with wet wings climb ladders to reach the upper stories.

The brass directory lists the name, talent, and room number of every fairy in Pixie Hollow.

The floor of the lobby is tiled with pearly mica. It took twenty masonry-talent fairies over two years to carry the mica in, piece by piece.

The lobby windows are made from reground pirate glass.

Talents

Beyond the lobby is a corridor lined with paintings. Each picture celebrates a different fairy talent. Talents are very important to the Never fairies. Fairies of the same talent work together, play together, eat together, and their fellow talent members are usually, but not always, their best friends. A fairy's greatest joy comes from performing her talent.

The feather you see here represents the pixie-dust-talent fairies. The acorn is for the tree-picking-talent fairies. The nose with half a mustache is the symbol for the coiffure-talent fairies. The wedge of cheese is for the cheese-making-talent fairies, a subtalent of the dairy fairies. Between main talents and subtalents, there are dozens upon dozens of different talents in Pixie Hollow.

Bedrooms

The fairies' bedrooms are on the upper stories of the Home Tree. Every fairy and sparrow man has his or her own private quarters here.

Every room is as unique as the fairy who lives there. When a new fairy arrives in Pixie Hollow, the decoration-talent fairies outfit her room in a way that best suits the fairy's talent and personality. A tree-bark-grading fairy's room might have a birch-bark canopy on the bed, while a water fairy's room would get woven seaweed curtains and sea-green walls.

The room pictured here belongs to a fairy named Prilla. Because her talent was a mystery at first, the decoration-talent fairies did not know what to do. So she received standard-issue fairy furniture, which is quite lovely nonetheless.

Fairies can be a bit vain. Most rooms come equipped with a full-length mirror so they may admire themselves.

TALENT: *Mainland-visiting clapping*

LIKES: *Playing with Clumsy children*

DISLIKES: *Feeling left out*

FAVORITE FOOD: *Poppy-puff rolls*

FAVORITE FLOWER: *Daisy*

Prilla

Prilla is one of the youngest fairies in Pixie Hollow. She is sweet-tempered, freckled, and pleasantly plump. Whenever she is happy—which is most of the time—she turns cartwheels or somersaults, or even does handsprings in the air.

Prilla has a talent unlike that of any other fairy in Never Land. In the blink of an eye, she can travel to the mainland—the world of Clumsies—where she visits children. She encourages them to clap to show they believe in fairies.

Prilla's talent is a result of the unusual laugh that formed her—there was an extra bit of Clumsy in the laugh that became Prilla. It took Prilla a long time to discover her talent. For a while she feared she might not have a talent at all. But Prilla's talent is one of the most important of all the Never fairies', for it keeps children's belief in fairies alive. It is so important, in fact, that many other talent groups have made her an honorary member so she will never feel alone.

A marble Prilla won in a game with a Clumsy child.

Prilla likes to wear her faux-mouse slippers.

Furnishings

Sycamore seeds make
simple ceiling fans.

Pillows are made from
flower petals and stuffed
with dandelion fluff.

Queen Clarion prefers Queen
Anne's lace curtains.

Spiderweb hammocks
are popular for relaxing.

A seashell chair belonging
to a water-talent fairy.

A dagger made from a pirate's toothpick.

Found Objects

The fairies found this odd long-handled brush in Havendish Stream. It turned out to be perfect for brushing squirrels' tails.

This horseshoe proved to be an excellent find for a garden-talent fairy.

Never fairies are extremely industrious and clever. In their world, nothing ever goes to waste. In fact, fairies have no word in their language for "useless."

Occasionally, items from the world of Clumsies will wash up on Never Land's shores. If found by fairies, these objects are always put to good use.

A thimble makes a fairy-sized bucket.

The Tearoom

The tearoom is a favorite gathering place for Never fairies, perhaps because of its serene atmosphere. The walls are papered with blades of pale Never grass, and the floor is always carpeted with fresh flowers.

Meal times in the tearoom are splendidly lavish. The tables are set with elegant maple-leaf linens. Table-setting-talent fairies arrange full place settings and fold the leaf napkins into a different shape each day. Polishing-talent fairies make sure every knife, fork, and spoon sparkles. Serving-talent fairies have a perfect sense of timing and always know when to bring out the next course or another pot of tea.

Menu

Barley crackers with mouse Brie
Chestnut dumpling soup

Acorn soufflé
Roast of mock turtle with thyme
Baked peas stuffed
with savory sesame puree

Fig-chocolate cake
Nutmeg pie

Honeysuckle nectar
Dew
Lemongrass tea

A sample fairy menu

The Kitchen

Directly off the tearoom is the kitchen, one of the busiest rooms in the Home Tree. Fairies from more than twenty-five different talents work here, including cooking, baking, and tea-making, along with many subtalents, such as bread buttering and salt sifting. With hundreds of fairies to cook for every day, the

larder-talent fairies keep the pantry well stocked. A pot hardly has a moment to be dirty before a scullery-talent fairy whisks it away.

A tree-bark side kitchen door leads outside. Many of the fairies who work outdoors deliver fresh ingredients directly from the gardens, orchard, and fields.

Fairy Foods

Most of the foods the fairies eat come straight from the garden fairies' gardens or from the surrounding forest. Fruits, nuts, mushrooms, seeds, and the occasional potato make up most of their diet. Fairies also keep a herd of dairy mice for milk, cheese, and butter. They season their food with sea salt, which is made from seawater collected on the far side of Never Land. Although the Mermaid Lagoon is closer, most fairies are wary of mermaid magic and find sea salt from the lagoon unfit for consumption.

Fairies always keep plenty of nutmeg seeds on hand to make nutmeg pie, a Never fairy favorite.

Despite their healthful diet, most Never fairies tend to have a sweet tooth.

Most fairies arrive with the knowledge of which mushrooms are safe to eat.

*Berries are a staple of
the fairy diet.*

Dulcie's Poppy-Puff Rolls

2 acorn capfuls mouse milk

1 hummingbird egg

1 large pinch sea salt

6 teaspoons sweet buttercup nectar

1 1/2 capfuls mouse butter, melted

5 capfuls hayseed flour

1 1/2 capfuls pulverized poppy seeds

1/2 tarragon leaf, finely chopped

Whisk milk, egg, salt, and buttercup nectar until blended.
Add melted butter and stir into mixture. Sift flour into
mixture one capful at a time. Sprinkle dough with pixie
dust, and allow it to knead itself until smooth.

Roll out dough into large rectangle. Sprinkle with poppy
seeds and tarragon. Cut into long strips, then roll the
strips into the shape of a snail shell. Bake in brick
oven. Remove when golden brown.

Makes 100 rolls

Fairies grow much of
their own food. They prefer
fresh fruit and vegetables
whenever possible.

The Library

Tucked into an out-of-the-way branch just above the kitchen is the Home Tree
library. Here the floor-to-ceiling shelves are filled with books on every imaginable
subject, from dragon anatomy to the folk songs of earthworms to the history
of pixie dust. A small group of scribe-talent fairies are constantly adding new
volumes to the shelves.

The library is a treasure trove of fairy knowledge. However, fairies are often so
busy with their own talents that they forget to visit this quiet room. Unlike other
parts of the Home Tree, it is never crowded and is always a peaceful place to read.

Leaf Lettering

A B C D E

F G H I J

K L M N O

P Q R S T

U V W Y Z

Fairies use quills or
wood splinters dipped
in berry ink to write.

The earliest written language known to the Never fairies is called Leaf Lettering. Each letter in this alphabet is composed of a symbol resembling a different kind of leaf. The Leaf alphabet has only 25 letters—there is no symbol for the letter we know as "x."

Never fairies are the only creatures who can read Leaf Lettering. In recent times, most fairies have abandoned it in favor of a more common alphabet that can be read by all literate citizens of Never Land, from mermaids to Peter Pan. But when a fairy needs to write a secret message that only other Never fairies may read, she will use the ancient Leaf alphabet. Fairies also use it when they want to be very formal. Because drawing each leaf symbol can be time-consuming, such correspondence is usually very short.

Ink is made from blackberries.

Workshops

The lower floors of the Home Tree house the workshops of many different talents, from keyhole-design fairies to carpenter fairies and everything in between.

Here is the workshop of Tinker Bell, a pots-and-pans-talent fairy. These fairies are responsible for repairing all the metal tools and utensils used in Pixie Hollow. When fixing a leaky pot, they can quickly discern whether it is a pinprick leak or a squiggle leak, an instant leak or a gradual one. Although they're usually busy fixing things like bent ladles or dented pots, they have a knack for working on anything made of metal.

Tinker Bell's workshop is made from a real Clumsy teakettle that washed up on the shores of Never Land. Tinker Bell shined it up and punched holes in the sides for doors and windows. She used pixie-dust magic to squeeze the entire teapot into the Home Tree. Note the awning over her door—it's actually the teakettle's spout, turned upside down.

Many metal-working fairies protect their eyes with goggles made from sea glass.

TALENT: *Pots-and-pans*

LIKES: *Fixing things, adventures, Peter Pan*

DISLIKES: *Things she can't fix, Vidia, gossip*

FAVORITE FOOD: *Pumpkin muffins*

FAVORITE FLOWER: *Silverbell*

Tinker Bell

She has a bounce when she lands, a curl to her ponytail, and lovely dimples when she smiles. She favors green leaf dresses, and she often carries a dagger on her belt. Her name is Tinker Bell, though most of her friends just call her Tink.

Tink is by far the best pots-and-pans fairy in Pixie Hollow. She's a problem solver and has a passion for fixing things. The toughest jobs are always her favorites.

Tink often faces tricky, rather magical repairs, such as colanders that have holes but will not drain, or circular tube pans that keep going oblong. Tink remembers each of her repairs fondly, almost as if they were old friends. She even keeps a portrait of a stockpot, a whisk, and a griddle over her bed.

Tink was once in love with the infamous Peter Pan. For a long time, in fact, she neglected her pots and pans for him. But Peter broke Tink's heart when he brought a Clumsy named Wendy to Never Land and paid more attention to her than to Tink. Soon after, Tink returned to tinkering, but she has never forgotten Peter.

Tink can be impatient, and she is easily annoyed. Yet there is no fairy more loyal or quick to fly to someone's rescue. No one could have a better friend than Tink.

Tink carries a finger harp in her pocket so she can always play a tune.

Tink rarely goes anywhere without her tinker's hammer, her most important tinkering tool.

The Sewing Room

Every Never fairy's wardrobe is as unique as the fairy who wears it. In a split second, measuring-talent fairies can size up the length of a fairy's arm or the circumference of her waist. Sewing-talent fairies then take care to design clothes that suit the fairy's talent. A water fairy's dress might have several pockets to hold extra leafkerchiefs. A scout-talent sparrow man's tunic would be made with greens and browns that blend into the forest, so he can spot predators before they spot him.

Never fairies make their clothes out of natural materials. Irises, daffodils, and roses are often used for elegant fashions. The smooth petals of foxglove are ideal for creating streamlined clothing for flying. Weaving-talent fairies also make cloth from beetle hair, spiderwebs, silkworm threads, thistledown, dandelion fluff, and caterpillar wool. Fairies are very creative and often use found objects in their clothing. Half a walnut shell might become a helmet for a tree-picking-talent fairy. A Lost Boy's lost button makes a fine base for a jaunty hat.

A formal gown made from spider silk and plum leaves. Rose petals and seed pearls are added for decoration.

Fairy Clothes

A flower parasol provides protection against sun and rain.

Rose petals create a delicately perfumed skirt.

Tulip slippers with rose pompoms are casual yet elegant.

The difficult work of mining requires durable clothing.

Their headgear comes with a firefly attachment.

Tough leaves from a Bimbim tree make a rugged tunic.

They wear sturdy beetle-shell boots.

Her bodice
is made from a
velvety rose petal.

The Queen's train is
made from
poinsettia petals.

Forget-me-not
bows adorn
her skirt.

Her tiered skirt is
made from champagne-
colored rose petals.

54

SHOES

Much of the time, fairy footwear never touches the ground. Cobbler-talent fairies custom-make all the footwear in Pixie Hollow, and each pair of shoes is a work of art. Some fairy footwear, such as shoes with pine-needle heels, is altogether too delicate for walking. When fairies aren't flying they'll opt for more comfortable footwear such as wasp skin boots or pussy-willow-pod moccasins.

The Laundry Room

Hidden away at the back of the Home Tree, behind the kitchen, is the laundry room. Here the laundry-talent fairies wash the clothes of all the fairies in Pixie Hollow.

A network of laundry chutes reaching all the way to the uppermost branches of the Home Tree empties the fairies' soiled clothing and linens into laundry baskets. Springwater from Havendish Stream comes into the room by means of a huge spigot that opens from one wall.

Since fairy clothing is very delicate, laundry-talent fairies hand wash every item. Once it is washed, the wet laundry is placed in balloon carriers—carts kept aloft by fairy-dust-filled balloons—which lift it up to the laundry lines where it can be hung to dry.

Bathing Branches

Tucked away on hidden branches of the Home Tree are the fairies' bathing rooms. Water for bathing must be carried in all the way from Havendish Stream and then heated. Bath-drawing-talent fairies are called on to help when a fairy wants a bath.

THE QUEEN'S TUB

The queen has her own bathtub in her quarters. Unlike the coconut-shell bathtubs most fairies use, hers is made of pewter. The notches in the back are where she rests her wings to keep them dry. The tub has morning-glory leaves sculpted into the sides, as fairies believe them to be a symbol of good health.

Fairy Hygiene

Fairy combs and hairbrushes are made from pine needles.

When they are away from the Home Tree, fairies find a bit of soapstone to wash their hands.

Fairies clean their teeth by chewing on peppermint leaves.

Orange blossom petals make fragrant washcloths.

Wing-washing Fairies

Wing cleaning is a difficult task. Since wings dry very slowly, it may be hours before a fairy with damp wings can fly again. The care of wings is usually left up to the wing-washing-talent fairies, who use special cloths made from the down of milk thistles. However, non-wing-washing-talent fairies may wash a friend's wings as a means of apology or a way of saying thank you. It is a special kindness to offer to wash another fairy's wings.

BEYOND
the Home Tree

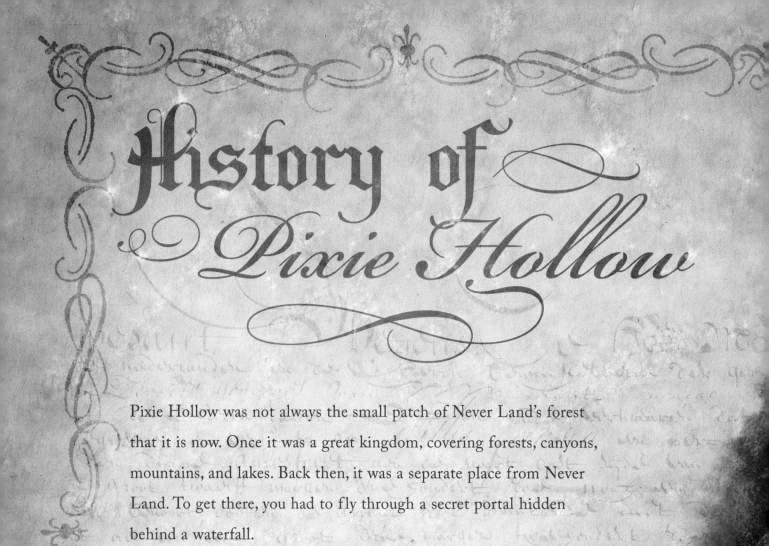

History of Pixie Hollow

Pixie Hollow was not always the small patch of Never Land's forest that it is now. Once it was a great kingdom, covering forests, canyons, mountains, and lakes. Back then, it was a separate place from Never Land. To get there, you had to fly through a secret portal hidden behind a waterfall.

At that time, the fairies made their homes in flowers, mushrooms, tree stumps, and other places all over Pixie Hollow. There was no Home Tree. In its place stood the Pixie Dust Tree. The charmed dust billowed endlessly from the heart of this enchanted tree, giving the fairies the magic they needed to travel to the world of children and inspire their belief.

The fairies lived this way happily for many years. Then came a battle that destroyed the Pixie Dust Tree. Pixie Hollow itself began to disappear, for without dust there could be no magic, and without magic there would be no belief in fairies. The fairies feared for their existence.

And then they found Mother Dove.

Mother Dove

Mother Dove is a magical creature and the closest thing to pure goodness in Never Land. She makes her nest in a hawthorn tree at the edge of Pixie Hollow. It was at the base of this tree that the fairies first found her, drawn by her goodness. Mother Dove restored magic to Never Land and brought life back to Pixie Hollow.

Mother Dove was once a bird like any other. Then a terrible fire swept Never Land, burning everything in its path. Sitting in her hawthorn tree, Mother Dove burned along with the rest of the island, but she was not hurt. Instead, she was transformed into a magical creature invested with great knowledge. She taught the fairies a new way of making pixie dust by grinding the magical feathers she shed each year at molting time.

Mother Dove knows each of the fairies by name, and she loves every one of them. They often come to her for guidance. But the fairies aren't the only ones who rely on Mother Dove. It is Mother Dove's egg that holds the secret to all of Never Land. Day in and day out she sits on it, making sure it comes to no harm—for as long as her egg stays well and whole, no creature in Never Land will ever grow old.

THE QUEST

Once, Mother Dove's egg was destroyed in a hurricane. To save Pixie Hollow—and all of Never Land—three fairies were sent on a perilous quest to restore the egg. They faced many dangers to collect three rare and valuable items: a mermaid's comb, a feather from the golden hawk, and Captain Hook's cigar holder. These they bartered with the wicked dragon, Kyto, in return for his help restoring the egg. The quest was successful, and once again, life returned to normal on the magical island.

Animal-Talent Fairies

Although Mother Dove is dear to all who live in Pixie Hollow, the ones who know and understand her best are the animal-talent fairies.

These fairies have the unique ability to speak with any animal in its native tongue, whether it be Raccoon, Bird, Tree Frog, or Squirrel. They are extremely sensitive and can "read" an animal's thoughts or emotions. They know when an animal is frightened or sick and can tend to its needs to help it feel better.

Like the animals they work with, animal-talent fairies have a keen sense of smell and excellent hearing. They are skilled trackers and are frequently called upon to help find fairies who have lost their way in the woods.

There are several different types of animal-talent fairies in Pixie Hollow, including many subtalents, such as caterpillar shearers, cricket whistlers, and butterfly herders. All animal-talent fairies are deeply integrated into Never Land's animal world and strive to keep it harmonious.

TALENT: *Speaking to animals*

LIKES: *Playing games,
caring for Mother Dove,
having adventures*

DISLIKES: *Disagreements*

FAVORITE FOOD: *Acorn flour pancakes*

FAVORITE FLOWER: *Dandelion*

Twitter, a hummingbird,
is Beck's good friend.

Beck

As one of the finest animal-talent fairies, Beck has the special job of caring for Mother Dove. She makes sure that Mother Dove has everything she needs so she never has to leave her nest or her precious egg. Curious and good-hearted, Beck can be a bit shy. In many ways she feels more comfortable with animals than she does with her fellow fairies. In fact, she sometimes wishes she were an animal herself!

Beck's ability to speak Bird without an accent impresses even other animal-talent fairies. Animals instinctively trust Beck. Even the most timid young chipmunk can be drawn out by her playful personality.

Although Beck loves spending time with her animal friends, she's very curious about the world beyond Pixie Hollow. When she sees flocks of birds fly past, migrating to and from unknown places, she often feels the urge to join them. Beck can often be found racing swallows or playing hide-and-seek with squirrels. But she has a serious side, too. She has been known to risk her own life to save an animal's.

Beck's special outfit from her last
Arrival Day anniversary.

Animal-Talent Tunnels

So long ago that only Mother Dove can remember, the animal-talent fairies built an elaborate system of underground tunnels on Never Land. This labyrinth of passages stretches for miles under every part of the island. Animal-talent fairies use them to get anywhere they need to without being seen and without setting foot outdoors.

The tunnels connect countless burrows, tree hollows, nests, and dens that have been abandoned by animals. Occasionally, though, they bump up against a den that is still in use. When this happens, the fairies use their understanding of animal behavior (plus, a great deal of tact) to negotiate passage. The tunnel network is constantly expanding as new pathways are added, both by fairies and by animals.

Every animal-talent fairy arrives in Never Land knowing the tunnels like the back of her own hand. To this day, the tunnel system remains a baffling maze to all other Never fairies.

The Mill

Not far from Mother Dove's hawthorn tree, on the banks of Havendish Stream, sits the dust mill. This is where the dust-talent fairies grind Mother Dove's old feathers into pixie dust.

The mill is built from peach pits. Its large double doors open into a work-room, where dust-talent fairies make separate piles of wing feathers, back feathers, neck feathers, and belly feathers, each of which has a different magical potency. It takes just the right amount of each kind of feather to make a perfect batch of pixie dust. Once they are sorted, the feathers are loaded into a hopper and fed through the grindstone.

The dust-talent fairies store the dust in canisters made from dried pumpkins. The fairies are very careful as they work. Pixie dust is so precious that they make sure not a single grain blows away.

When dust-talent fairies aren't using the mill, the tree pickers use it to grind acorns into flour.

Terence

Terence has one of the most important jobs in Pixie Hollow. Each day, he rises before dawn to help hand out pixie dust to the other fairies. Fairies need one level teacup of dust each day in order to fly and do magic.

Terence is charming, calm, and kind. Because of his work, he also tends to be quite dusty. Pixie dust powders his hair and clings to his coat. As a result, he sparkles more than the average sparrow man.

A curious characteristic of dust-talent fairies is that they never, ever sneeze. They cannot risk blowing away any valuable fairy dust.

Terence has a bit of a crush on Tinker Bell (which every fairy in Pixie Hollow knows except for Tink herself). He's always dropping by Tink's workshop with a pot or kettle that needs fixing. Although Tink is unaware of his crush on her, she considers him a dear friend.

A poem Terence wrote for Tinker Bell.

For Tink

Courageous as the day is long,

Magic as a mermaid's song,

Honest as an ocean breeze,

Tender as a cuddle vine's squeeze.

But here I've just begun to tell

The wondrous charms of Tinker Bell.

Terence carries a teacup for measuring out fairy dust.

TALENT: *Pixie dust*

LIKES: *Knickknacks (he loves how they collect dust), Tinker Bell*

DISLIKES: *Oversleeping*

FAVORITE FOOD: *Strawberry cake*

FAVORITE GAME: *Tag*

Havendish Stream

Water-Talent Fairies

Downstream from the dust mill, Havendish Stream branches into a network of canals where the water fairies like to play.

Water-talent fairies can manipulate water in astonishing ways. They can mold it like clay, make it freeze or boil, or create powerful waves in puddles and ponds with just a flick of pixie dust.

Water fairies are often found exploring Pixie Hollow's waterways in boats made from leaves and in birch-bark canoes. These fairies also have a knack for divining and can seek out hidden sources of water. Only water-talent fairies can make bubble messages, which burst open only for the fairy who is meant to hear them.

The most emotional of the Never fairies, water fairies cry when they're happy as well as when they're sad. But they can hardly be blamed. They are so full of water their tears spill easily.

Although water fairies cannot swim, they always find ways to frolic near water.

TALENT: *Water*

LIKES: *Swimming*

DISLIKES: *Deserts*

FAVORITE FOOD: *Watermelon ice*

FAVORITE FLOWER: *Water lily*

*Rani rides on Brother Dove's
back when she needs to fly.*

Rani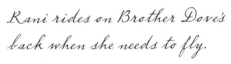

Of all the water-talent fairies, Rani is the most passionate. She loves rainy days and splashing in puddles. She even knows how to whistle mermaid songs. Her favorite dreams are swimming dreams.

Rani can do amazing, magical things with water: bounce it like a ball, mold it into the shape of a fish, or scoop it up in her fingers without losing a drop. She can also help her fellow fairies with water-related things, such as getting water to boil faster.

Rani is the only fairy in Pixie Hollow who can swim. This is because she has no wings—she sacrificed them on the Quest to save Mother Dove's egg. She's not entirely unhappy about losing her wings, since she had always longed to swim, though she misses being able to fly on her own.

Now Rani flies with the help of Brother Dove. Whenever she needs him, Rani whistles, and Brother flies to her side and carries her wherever she needs to go.

*Rani treasures the shell
Silvermist gave her on her
first day in Never Land.*

The Meadow

To one side of Havendish Stream lies the meadow where the fairies take their herds of caterpillars, butterflies, and dairy mice to pasture. The fairies keep mice for their milk and wool. Woolly caterpillars are also raised for their fur, while butterflies lay the eggs that become caterpillars.

Though the herd of butterflies is quite large, over fifty in number, there are few butterfly herders among the Never fairies. Butterflies are very intelligent and extremely mischievous by nature. The butterfly herders are the only fairies with the patience to work with these obnoxious critters.

Caterpillar-shearing-talent fairies are also frequently seen in the meadow. When the caterpillars' coats are thick and fluffy, these fairies go to work. The wool is turned into blankets, pillows, and extrawarm sweaters by weaving-talent fairies.

On the other side of Havendish Stream from the meadow lies the orchard where the tree-picking talents work. These fairies and sparrow men possess a keen sense of smell, which helps them know exactly when a fruit or nut is ripe and ready to be picked. They also have excellent balance, which allows them to easily carry large loads of fresh fruit on their heads.

While harvest-talent fairies gather all manner of berries, seeds, shoots, flower nectar, and mushrooms, the tree-picking fairies specialize in the more difficult job of pulling large fruits and nuts from trees. Their work is very dangerous—more than one tree picker has narrowly missed being squashed by a falling apple or pomegranate. They usually wear protective headgear and carry heavy tools to help them detach thick-stemmed fruit from tree branches.

The Orchard.

One tree the harvest-talent fairies avoid is the sour-plum tree at the far end of the orchard. While its shiny purple fruit look enticing, they have an extremely sour flavor that makes all but the toughest taste buds pucker. Fairies, birds, animals, and insects are also deterred from picking the fruit by the sour disposition of the tree's sole inhabitant—Vidia.

TALENT:	*Fast-flying*
LIKES:	*Being the fastest, making mean remarks*
DISLIKES:	*Poppy seeds, dandelions, almost all other fairies*
FAVORITE FOOD:	*Lemon tart*
FAVORITE FLOWER:	*Prickly pear blossom*

*Vidia likes to race
dragonflies when the other
fairies aren't looking.*

Vidia

Vidia is the fastest of the fast-flying-talent fairies. Her love for flying—and her greed for speed—is so strong that she'll stop at nothing to be faster. In hopes of making more powerful fairy dust, Vidia once plucked ten feathers from Mother Dove before a scout caught her. Ever since Vidia stole the feathers, Queen Clarion has banned her from Mother Dove's presence.

Vidia delights in making cruel remarks and seeing the shocked looks on other fairies' faces. She uses sugary phrases, such as "darling" and "dear" when addressing other fairies, though everyone knows she doesn't mean them. Her desire for speed also makes her impatient; she gets angry when other fairies hold her up.

When it comes to her attire, Vidia likes to keep things light. She wears featherweight clothing, such as hummingbird-down vests and leggings made from woven dandelion silk.

*Vidia keeps her "fresh"
fairy dust locked in a
box, which she hides
under her bed.*

Garden-Talent Fairies

Like harvest- and tree-picking-talent fairies, garden fairies spend most of their time outdoors. Their colorful gardens can be seen in all corners of Pixie Hollow.

Garden-talent fairies have a special relationship with all things that grow from the earth. They can sense what a plant needs and have an intuitive understanding of how to help it blossom and grow.

They feel as close to plants as animal-talent fairies feel to animals. But garden fairies have been known to work with animals, too. They sometimes train earthworms and ladybugs to help them, and they are highly respectful of bumblebees.

TALENT: *Gardening*

LIKES: *Watching the grass grow*

DISLIKES: *Being away from her garden*

FAVORITE FOOD: *Ever fruit*

FAVORITE FLOWER: *She loves them all!*

*Bumble is Lily's
dear friend.*

Lily

One of the most beautiful gardens in Pixie Hollow belongs to Lily. She always tends to her plants with great love and care. She can sense whether her plants feel content or troubled, thirsty or hungry, safe or threatened. She wraps the most delicate plants with silk on cool evenings and brings them extra water on hot days. No matter how big or small, she wants all her plants to be happy.

With her sparkling eyes and friendly smile, Lily is as lovely as the flowers that bloom in her garden. Yet she is very down-to-earth and practical. Lily sometimes goes barefoot to feel the soil between her toes. She's one of the few fairies who prefers walking to flying. On sunny days, she's never without her daisy-petal sun hat.

Lily is also extremely patient. She understands that time passes at a different pace for plants than it does for animals or fairies. One of her favorite things to do is to lie in a patch of grass and watch the blades grow. Like all plants, the grass thrives in Lily's company—it grows faster when she's watching.

*This is Lily's favorite
watering can.*

Pixie Hollow Flora

In addition to many common herbs and flowers, the garden fairies' gardens are home to a number of unusual plants.

The **EVER TREE** is not actually a tree, but a large flowering plant. It blooms only once, then bears fruit forever— a fruit plucked from its branches will immediately grow back. Ever trees once covered Never Land. Now the only known Ever tree grows in Pixie Hollow.

One of the shyest plants is the **POSSUM FERN.** If it detects danger, it will play dead by uncoiling its leaves and turning brown. It grows mainly in parts of the woods where few creatures wander, though the occasional garden fairy has managed to coax one to grow in her garden.

Despite its sharp needles, the **RAINDROP CACTUS** is a handy plant to have around. It "sweats" beads of rain, which can be collected in buckets. The liquid is clear like dew. It is quite delicious all by itself, or as a tasty addition to soups and stews.

The **CUDDLE VINE** will grab hold of anyone or anything that passes within reach of its long, spindly vines. It is not a dangerous plant, though a fairy who has been caught may find it difficult to get untwined from its amorous green arms.

The garden-talent fairy Iris keeps a journal of all the plants in Never Land. Although she has no garden of her own, Iris knows more about plants than almost any fairy in Pixie Hollow. (Turn the page for a look inside IRIS'S JOURNAL.)

BUTTERCUPS

I got this tip from a Tiffen. To get the biggest, sunniest buttercups, you must baste them with real butter — at least two cups each day.

NOTE:
Buttercups make delicious soup.

SPRINTING THISTLE

One of the healthiest, heartiest plants in Never Land, this thistle can extract itself from the ground and run about on its roots. This is a great advantage for the thistle, which can take itself to water or sunlight. It can also outrun predators. No fairy has ever succeeded in domesticating a sprinting thistle.

Fairy Remedies

The garden fairies provide more than just food to the fairies of Pixie Hollow. They also grow herbs and other plants, which the healing-talent fairies use to make medicine to treat all kinds of ailments.

HAZY OR SHADOWY GLOWS

1 sunflower seed, crushed
3 fireweed petals, grated
A sprinkling of goldenseal pollen

Mix sunflower seed and fireweed petals until well blended. Fold in goldenseal. Use as a scrub mornings and evenings for three days.

*A healing-talent fairy
tends to a sick firefly.*

FLUTTERING FLIGHT

1 scoop dandelion fluff
5 hawkweed hairs, ground
3 speedwell petals, minced

Mix all ingredients. Add to daily
sprinkling of fairy dust until flight
patterns are back to normal.

BUG BITES OR SUNBURN

1 drop aloe juice
5 drops milkweed sap, chilled

Stir chilled milkweed sap into aloe
juice until thick and creamy. Smooth
over affected areas.

FAIRY POX

1 pinch daisy pollen

Take one dose of daisy pollen daily
until symptoms disappear.

FAIRY FLU

3 rosehips, dried and ground

Dissolve in hot sassafras tea and
drink. Take three times daily.

✚ Nursing-Talent Fairies

Unlike healing-talent fairies, who mostly mix potions, nursing-talent fairies deal with scrapes, cuts, and broken bones. They have a magic touch and can take the sting out of small wounds simply by blowing on them.

There is a sick bay in the Home Tree where nursing fairies tend to those who need extended bed rest. Flying collisions occasionally result in bumps on the head that need a soothing skullcap-and-comfrey compress. Broken bones are set with cactus spines and cloth bandages.

Dangers to Fairies.

Although fairies do not age, they are not, as some believe, immortal.
They can fall victim to illness or predators.

WASPS do not prey on fairies, but like bees, they can be dangerous if accidentally agitated. They are as big as a Never fairy's head, and a single sting can be fatal to a fairy.

HAWKS are common in Never Land and pose a great threat to fairies. Although most hawks prefer to eat rodents, they are not above snatching up a fairy if they are particularly hungry. Despite this, animal-talent fairies respect them greatly for their dignity and grace.

DISBELIEF

Disbelief is the greatest threat to all fairies. The moment a single Clumsy child stops believing in them, fairies begin to fade and may die. The only thing that can save a dying Never fairy is the clapping of children who still believe.

With their powerful jaws and lightning speed, **SNAKES** are fearsome predators. Even the most skilled scouts would have difficulty overcoming an attacking snake. Most fairies quickly learn to avoid the flat, rocky cliffs where snakes like to sun. They look closely for tree snakes before landing in unfamiliar trees. Some animal-talent fairies are capable of lulling an angry snake back into a peaceful state, though they are careful to do so from a good distance.

Scouts

Scouts are among the bravest of all fairies. They are responsible for staying on the lookout for predators and warning other fairies if one is near. They may even risk their own lives to keep a fellow fairy from harm.

The scout's sharp eyesight rivals that of a hawk. They wear clothing that helps them blend into their hiding places and have learned to dim their glows to keep from being spotted. Although they carry quivers of arrows made from saw grass or porcupine quills, they only shoot in self-defense or to protect other fairies.

Using slivers of bluegrass between their thumbs, scouts relay messages to each other over distances farther than their voices can carry. Three quick shrills indicate a circling hawk; one long shrill means all is well.

Fairy Amusements

Never fairies are naturally hardworking. They love their talents, so their work is also their greatest joy. But after a long day spent laboring, they always take time to frolic, dance, sing, laugh, or compete in some of the many fairy games.

FAIRY TAG is played in the air, rather than on the ground. In this game, all the fairies in a talent become a team. A fairy is tagged by tapping her on the head and saying the words "Choose you." At that point, her entire talent group becomes "it." Every talent gets into the mix, each time coming up with new ways to outfox the fairies in another group. The fairies use every trick and bit of magic to try and win.

Light-talent fairies throw beams of light back into the eyes of the fairies chasing them.

The water-talent fairies have been tagged "it." They try to catch their opponents by hurling balls of water at their wings.

The animal-talent fairies recruit help from the chipmunks.

There are no set rules for BUTTERFLY RACES. In this game, each player chooses a butterfly. A finish line is then agreed on—usually a flower or puddle at some distance. The fairy or sparrow man whose butterfly makes it to the finish line first is the winner. Of course, butterflies never fly in a straight line, nor do they pay any attention whatsoever to the cheers or encouragement of fairies. These willful creatures fly wherever they want, so the fairies must use clever tactics—such as casting shadows of large birds—to chase their butterflies toward the finish line.

Fairies also enjoy a good
practical joke, such as magically
decorating an unsuspecting
friend with polka dots.

Art-Talent Fairies

Some of the liveliest fairies in Pixie Hollow are the art talents. They specialize in many different kinds of art, including painting, sculpting, woodworking, glass-blowing. . . . There are even fairies who make art with stray bits of sunlight.

These fairies have the good fortune of finding inspiration in everything, and they make creative use of whatever they find. Bess, an art-talent fairy, has cleverly transformed this tangerine crate into a painting studio.

TALENT: *Painting*

LIKES: *Sharing her work*

DISLIKES: *Criticism*

FAVORITE FOOD: *Blueberry pie*

FAVORITE FLOWER: *Tulip*

Bess's favorite paintbrushes are made from vole hairs.

Bess

Bess is a bit messy—she usually has paint splattered on her hands, her clothing, and even sometimes in her hair. Her studio is cluttered with easels, jars of linseed oil, brushes of all sizes, and paint-making supplies. But since she is Pixie Hollow's most talented painter, no one pays much mind to her messy clothes or crowded studio.

Bess keeps a large sketchbook filled with sketches inspired by daily life. Magically, the pages in Bess's sketchbook never run out—she's had the same one since she first arrived in Pixie Hollow. She loves sharing her work with the other fairies, although she is quite sensitive to criticism.

Bess is the official portrait artist for Mother Dove. Much of her finest work decorates the walls of the Home Tree, and large murals can be found throughout the fairy world bearing her signature.

Bess's first portrait of Mother Dove.

One of the most colorful events to take place in the courtyard is DYEING DAY. When the last of Pixie Hollow's nuts and fruits have been harvested, dyeing-talent fairies gear up for their most important day of the year. With help from the water fairies, they boil roots, bark, blueberries, beets, dandelions, black-berries, and certain kinds of grass to create dyes in every color of the rainbow.

Fairies hang dyed leaves
and clothes out to dry.

Sparrow men
prepare a beet
to make dye.

Every few seasons, all the fairies in Pixie Hollow come together for GREAT GAMES DAY. On this day, fairies compete against other members of their talent group in specialized games. Events include the Potato Heft, the Carrot Toss (much like a javelin contest), Swift Diving, Leapfrog Races, Water Skating (in which water-talent fairies gracefully glide over the surfaces of still ponds or puddles), and a Fast-Flying Race. Since fairies dislike being bound by rules, they often make them up as they go along.

Fairies love listening to story-
talent fairies tell stories.

Percussionists play drums made from hollowed-out minipumpkins.

Music

Never fairy music is joyful and lively. Whenever music-talent fairies play, other fairies cannot help but join in by singing and dancing.

A chirping chorus of crickets, led by
the cricket-whistling-talent fairies,
often accompanies the musicians.

Songs

"FLY NOT FAR FROM ME"

*Come fly with me to Pixie Hollow
where the Never fairies follow
the way to the hawthorn tree*

*Fly not far…
Fly not far…
Fly not far from me*

*I'll fly with you to the fairy circle
where our wings will sparkle
with Mother Dove's love*

*Fly not far…
Fly not far…
Fly not far from me*

*But if one day you slip away
because of disbelief
I'll fly for you, I'll cry for you
I'll fly backward if I can*

*So, fly not far…
Fly not far…
Fly not far from me*

Wind instruments played by music fairies include shell horns, reed-grass flutes, and trumpet flowers.

"ARRIVAL DAY SONG"

*Hurray, hurray for Arrival Day
Hurray, hurray for Arrival Day*

*You are born from laughter
And a Never fairy ever after
From the first sprinkling of dust
You'll have magic you can trust*

*Hurray, hurray for Arrival Day
Hurray, hurray for Arrival Day*

Non-music-talent fairies also enjoy making music. Water fairies create complex melodies with plinks, trickles, drips, and splashes.

Pixie Hollow
AT NIGHT

Light-Talent Fairies

By far the brightest creatures in Never Land are the light-talent fairies. They are the stars of celebratory light shows and put on dazzling performances. At these times, their glows are so brilliant that Clumsy sailors out on the ocean have mistaken them for lightning on the horizon.

Unlike other creatures, light-talent fairies can look directly at the sun without burning their eyes. They have an instinctual understanding of the constellations and are expert navigators. The phases of the moon greatly influence light fairies' ability to do magic. Their skills are more powerful during a full moon and are at their weakest during a new moon.

Light fairies are responsible for keeping Pixie Hollow aglow once the sun sets. They train fireflies and glowworms to work as torches and lanterns. During emergencies, such as a firefly no-fire flu epidemic, light-talent fairies work overtime to light up Pixie Hollow with their own glows. After such intense glowing, light fairies need much rest to regain their normal radiance.

TALENT: *Light*

LIKES: *Napping in the sun*

DISLIKES: *Cloudy days, waking early*

FAVORITE FOOD: *Sunflower seed soufflé*

FAVORITE FLOWER: *Sunflowers*

One of Fira's trained fireflies.

Fira

Fira's personality is as fiery and dynamic as her glow. As the strongest of the light-talent fairies, she is a natural leader. Fira is responsible for training all the fireflies that light Pixie Hollow at night. She is irresistibly drawn toward any light source, so it's no wonder her friends have given her the nickname Moth.

Fira loves to take charge. During light shows, she is the main choreographer. She also teaches other light fairies the best way to wrangle glowworms and fireflies.

Fira has a tendency to think that if something is going to be done right, she must do it herself. Her desire to be in charge can backfire on her sometimes, causing her to forget to rely on the talents of her fellow fairies. She often works harder than is necessary and tires herself out too quickly. After a hard day's work, Fira regains her strength by taking a catnap in a sunny patch of Lily's garden, or by moonbathing on a high branch in the Home Tree.

Fira's astronomy book.
It's open to the drawing of
her favorite constellation.

The Molt

Once a year, Mother Dove gets the pre-Molt tingles. That familiar feeling means it's time for her to shed her old feathers, which she passes on to the Never fairies to turn into pixie dust. The Molt is a time for rejoicing and is accompanied by a grand celebration with music, entertainment, and feasting.

As the Molt draws near, the fairies make sure everything is in tip-top shape. The windows in the Home Tree sparkle, the laundry is pressed and put away, and the tables are set for an outdoor banquet. By twilight, fairies dressed in their finest fill the branches of the hawthorn tree where Mother Dove's nest sits. The moment before the festivities begin, whispers quiet to a hush, and fairies lower their glows in anticipation.

Light-talent fairies start off the evening with a tribute to Mother Dove in the form of a light show. The dancing points of light they create resemble the flames of a fire. Their dance is meant to represent the fire that created Mother Dove.

When the light show is over, the fairy queen makes her annual speech. Perched atop Mother Dove's head, she reflects on how the year has been for the fairies. The fairies toast to the year's blessings and triumphs. Soon after, Bess's latest portrait of Mother Dove is unveiled, and the fairies sit down to a nine-course banquet.

Mother Dove's pre-Molt tingle continues to gain strength throughout the evening. At last, her feathers fall. The Molt is complete, and there is blessed peace in Pixie Hollow.

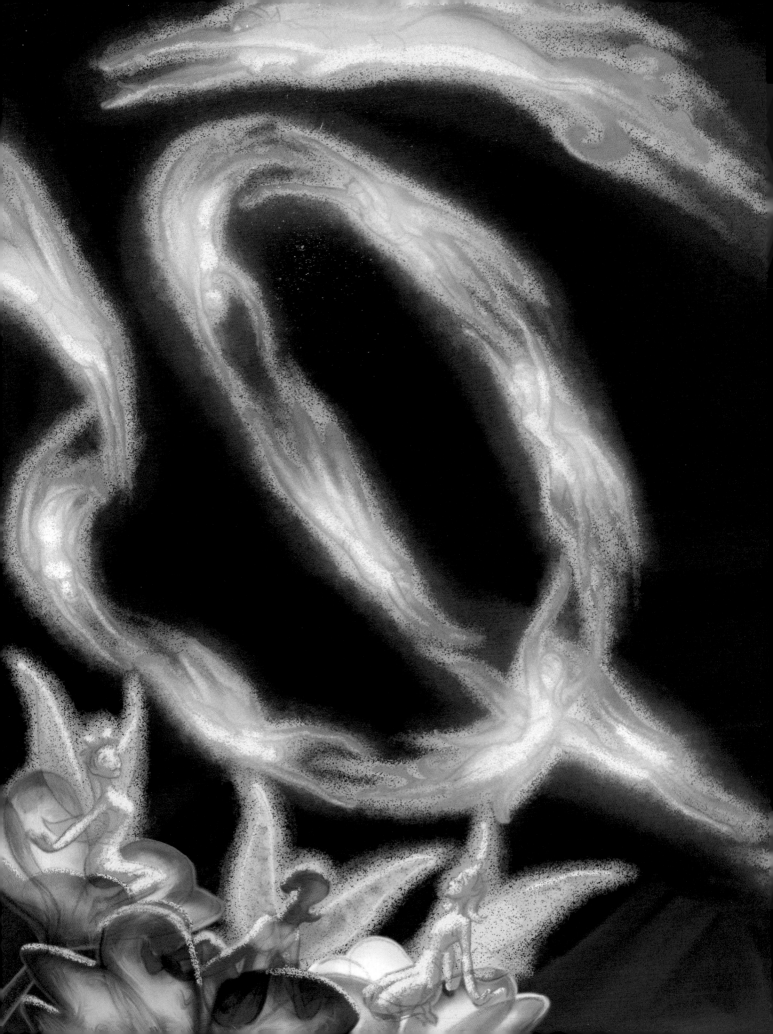

The Fairy Dance

When the moon is at its fattest, brightest, and merriest, the Never fairies gather in the fairy circle, the ring of mushrooms near Mother Dove's hawthorn tree. Then they begin the Fairy Dance. This airborne dance is very complicated—only fairies can understand its choreography.

No matter the time of year or day in Pixie Hollow, there is always a Never fairy or sparrow man doing what she or he loves best. Whatever their talents may be, all fairies bring a unique joy that adds to the magic of Pixie Hollow. As long as babies keep laughing and children keep clapping, Mother Dove will continue to sit on her precious blue egg. The pixie-dust mill will continue to churn. And Never fairies will never, ever stop flying.